Tonight at Nine

Tonight at Nine

JANOSCH

Henry Z. Walck, Incorporated   *New York*

The rooster crows with all his might:
"A concert will be held tonight.
Behind the barn, tonight at nine—
But only if the weather's fine."

First, hear the sound of rumbling drums.
Across the meadow Bruno comes.
And as he briskly trots along,
He barks aloud his marching song.

Behind him comes a big white bird,
As Lily Goose's flute is heard.
And while she makes this gentle sound,
She taps her feet and spins around.

Much later, in the afternoon,
The farmer Friedel plays his tune,
And round his head a butterfly
Dances with joy against the sky.

Now in this picture you can see
Matilda and her friend the bee.
Accordions are hard to play,
So she rehearses all the day.

"Tantantara." The trumpet clear
Rings out for everyone to hear.
"Tantantara," plays Greta Goat,
And Peep the bird loves every note.

Peter the blackbird sings all day,
Chirping his cheerful roundelay.
While he pours music from his beak,
Katie can only grunt, "Queek, queek."

Franz the conductor waves his tail.
He sees the light begin to fail,
And knows the time is getting late.
He gallops quickly to the gate.

The players put themselves in line,
Ready to start; it's nearly nine.
Gaily they sing and dance, and play
Their concert at the close of day.

While high above the meadow green,
The Man in the Moon is clearly seen.
He smiles and stretches out his hand
To hear the music of the band.

But when the sun climbs up the sky,
He laughs to see the players lie
All fast asleep, their music done;
"When's the next concert?" asks the sun.